# Unicorn School

# The Pet Show

## Linda Chapman

*Illustrated by Ann Kronheimer*

**PUFFIN**

PUFFIN BOOKS

Published by the Penguin Group
Penguin Books Ltd, 80 Strand, London WC2R ORL, England
Penguin Group (USA) Inc., 375 Hudson Street, New York, New York 10014, USA
Penguin Group (Canada), 90 Eglinton Avenue East, Suite 700, Toronto, Ontario, Canada M4P 2Y3
(a division of Pearson Penguin Canada Inc.)
Penguin Ireland, 25 St Stephen's Green, Dublin 2, Ireland (a division of Penguin Books Ltd)
Penguin Group (Australia), 250 Camberwell Road, Camberwell, Victoria 3124, Australia
(a division of Pearson Australia Group Pty Ltd)
Penguin Books India Pvt Ltd, 11 Community Centre, Panchsheel Park, New Delhi – 110 017, India
Penguin Group (NZ), 67 Apollo Drive, Rosedale, North Shore 0632, New Zealand
(a division of Pearson New Zealand Ltd)
Penguin Books (South Africa) (Pty) Ltd, 24 Sturdee Avenue, Rosebank,
Johannesburg 2196, South Africa

Penguin Books Ltd, Registered Offices: 80 Strand, London WC2R ORL, England

puffinbooks.com

First published 2008
1

Text copyright © Working Partners Ltd, 2008
Illustrations copyright © Ann Kronheimer, 2008
All rights reserved

The moral right of the author and illustrator has been asserted

Set in Bembo
Typeset by Palimpsest Book Production Limited. Grangemouth, Stirlingshire
Made and printed in England by Clays Ltd, St Ives plc

British Library Cataloguing in Publication Data
A CIP catalogue record for this book is available from the British Library

ISBN: 978-0-141-32251-3

www.greenpenguin.co.uk

*To James Wallace*

# ARCADIA

Sea of Silence

Cloud
Stables

Rose Quartz
Cliffs

Beach

Moonlight
Meadow

The Telling
Tree

Assembly
Fields

UNICORN SCHOOL

High Winds Pass

Bramble Forest

Flying Heath

Charm Fields

N
W
E
S

# Contents

# Chapter One

# Exciting News!

'Can't catch me!' Willow whinnied. Storm raced towards her. Willow plunged away, the sunlight glinting on her silver horn.

By the time Storm had swung round, Willow was already on the other side of the meadow. She liked playing tag! She was very good at it because she was small for her age and could turn easily.

Giving up on chasing Willow, Storm galloped after Troy instead.

Happiness fizzed through Willow as she watched them charging along the grass. She loved being at Unicorn School and spending so much time with her friends. All the unicorns who lived in the magic land of Arcadia went to Unicorn School when they were nine. They ate together, slept in cloud stables together and went to lessons together. It was great fun!

Suddenly she heard a whinny from behind her. She looked round. Sapphire, their other friend, was galloping towards them, her ears pricked.

'I've just heard some exciting news,' Sapphire neighed.

'What?' demanded Willow.

Leaving their game of tag, Storm and Troy cantered over.

'Oriel just told me that the Tricorn's going to make an

announcement at supper tonight,' panted Sapphire. 'No one knows what it is about yet but it sounds like it could be fun!'

Storm looked at Troy. 'Have you heard anything about it, Troy?'

Troy was a royal unicorn. His father was the king of Arcadia and the Tricorn, the school's headmaster, was his uncle.

Troy shook his head. 'Maybe the Tricorn's going to say we're about to have a sports day,' he said hopefully. He loved sports.

'Or we could be having a magic competition,' said Storm.

'Or putting on another play,' said Willow.

'Or maybe we're going to have a fancy-dress competition,' said Sapphire.

Just then, a horn blew signalling the end of lunchtime. Willow, Sapphire, Storm and Troy headed out of the meadows and up on to Weathertop Hill – a low mountain covered with purple flowers near the Flying Heath where they had their weather magic lessons.

Elderflower, the tall thin teacher,

was waiting for them. 'Today I'm going to teach you how to magic away fog,' she said as the Year Ones gathered round her.

Willow listened very carefully as Elderflower explained.

'It is very hard to clear away a fog completely,' Elderflower told them. 'You won't learn that sort of magic until you are older. For now, you will simply learn to clear a path through fog. To do this, you need a moonflower.' She picked one of the purple flowers from the ground. 'You must throw the moonflower into the fog and –' She broke off. 'Sapphire! Storm! Will you please stop talking!'

Willow felt her two friends jump beside her.

'Sorry, Elderflower,' they both muttered.

Elderflower continued. 'You throw the moonflower into the air and quickly draw a big circle round it with your horn. As you do this you must imagine the circle turning into a hole in the fog. As the moonflower touches the ground the fog should clear away in the circle you have drawn and you will be able to see ahead of you. All pick a moonflower and have a try.'

The Year Ones all quickly picked one of the purple flowers. When they each had one, Elderflower waved her horn in the air and a fog fell over the hill. It was thick and grey and cold. Willow stepped to the side and bumped into someone.

'Ow!' exclaimed Sapphire.

'Sorry!' gasped Willow.

Elderflower's voice floated to them through the fog. 'Use your magic to clear a path, everyone.'

Willow threw her moonflower in the air and quickly drew a circle round it with her horn. To her delight the air inside the circle she had drawn started to clear. It was like a tunnel appearing in the fog. She began to walk along it and emerged near the bottom of the hill.

'Well done, Willow!' Elderflower exclaimed. 'You're the first one out!'

Willow glowed with happiness. She loved learning new magic. As she waited for the others to find their way through the fog too, she thought about the announcement the Tricorn was going to make at supper and wondered what it could be.

# Chapter Two

# The Tricorn's Announcement

Meals at Unicorn School were always served in Moonshine Meadows. The unicorns ate at four long tables. There were holes in the tables for their feed buckets. That night it was oats, bran and barley with chopped-up apples for supper. It was one of Willow's favourite meals and she gobbled it so quickly, in anticipation of what the Tricorn was going to tell them, she ended up giving herself a tummy-ache.

At the end of the meal a wise-looking unicorn with a horn striped in bronze, silver and gold walked into the meadows. It was the Tricorn. An immediate hush fell.

'Good evening, everyone,' he said. 'As you may have heard, I have some news for you. The teachers have been telling me how hard you have been working this term and to reward you I have decided that next weekend we will hold a pet show!'

'A pet show!' Troy and several other unicorns cried.

'That's great!' Willow gasped to
Sapphire. Every unicorn in the land
had their own family pet. It sounded
like the perfect way of showing
them off!

Oriel, a Year Three unicorn, raised
his horn.

'Yes, Oriel?' the Tricorn said.

'How can we have a pet show
when all our pets are at home?' he
asked.

'Good point,' the Tricorn bowed

his head. 'I have sent letters to your parents and for those that want to enter the show, they will bring your pets along to school on Saturday. We will have a garden party at the same time and afterwards your parents will take your pets home again.'

A buzz of excitement rose.

'I am glad you all seem pleased by the news,' the Tricorn said, a smile in his voice. 'Now, here are the rules – you may each enter your pet for just one class and the winners of each class will compete for the prize of best pet in the show at the end of the day. It is up to you to decide which class you would like to enter. The list of classes will be put up on the Telling Tree tomorrow morning and the entry forms will be in the elfmail office. Please fill them in by Wednesday lunchtime.' His eyes twinkled. 'I hope you enjoy deciding which class to enter.' And with that, the Tricorn left the meadows.

'We'll get to see each other's pets!' said Troy as everyone started talking at once.

'You've got a giant butterfly, haven't you, Sapphire?' said Storm.

Sapphire nodded. 'She's called Flutter. She's got huge wings, as big as my hooves, and they are all different shades of purple and pink. I hope there's a class for the most beautiful pet.'

'I hope there's one for the pet who can sing the best or who's really fast,' said Willow, whose pet was a tiny hummingbird called Whizzy.

'What pet have you got, Troy?' Oriel called from further down the table.

'A mountain panther,' said Troy proudly. 'He's called Jet. He's got a black coat and a white circle on it that gets bigger and smaller to match the moon when it changes shape at night.'

'Wow!' said Oriel, impressed. 'I don't know anyone else who's got a mountain panther. If there's a class for the most unusual pet, you're bound to win.'

'I don't *think* so,' a Year Five unicorn, Azure, whinnied shrilly. She was slim with light brown eyes and looked down her long nose at the others.

Willow exchanged looks with her friends. None of them liked Azure very much because she had once been horrible to Troy.

'What pet have you got, Azure?' Oriel asked.

Azure looked very smug. 'I've got a magic fox!'

'A magic fox!' Troy echoed. 'But they're really difficult to keep as pets. They are very crafty and they get into all sorts of trouble.'

'They're the cleverest type of pet there is,' said Azure. 'They can change shape *and* start fires by banging their tails on the ground and they're very intelligent. I bet mine is going to win best pet in the show!' Azure declared. She walked away, her nose in the air.

Troy looked round at the others. 'It's amazing Azure's got a magic fox. I've never heard of anyone at school having one as a pet before. What have you got, Oriel?'

'A flying squirrel,' Oriel answered. 'He's got a bright red coat and he can fly from tree to tree.' He turned to Sapphire and said teasingly, 'What can your butterfly do, Sapphire? Or does she just look pretty?'

'No. She can do loads,' Sapphire said defensively. 'She can . . .' Sapphire hesitated. 'She can make flowers change colour when she lands on them.'

'Wow! That's pretty cool,' said Oriel. 'So, Troy's got a mountain panther with a moon on its coat, Sapphire's got a butterfly that can change the colours of flowers, I've got a flying squirrel and Azure's got a magic fox. How about your pet, Willow? What does he do?'

Willow paused. Everyone else's pets sounded amazing. What would they think if she said that all that Whizzy could do was sing? 'He . . . he can fly so fast you can't see him,' she said quickly. She saw Oriel's eyes widen. She knew she shouldn't have said it because it wasn't true. Whizzy *could* fly fast but not so fast that he turned invisible. It was just that everyone else's pets had sounded so cool!

Before Oriel could ask her anything more about Whizzy, Willow turned hastily to Storm. 'You're being quiet,' she said, nudging him with her horn. 'What's Archie good at?'

Storm kept a photo of Archie – his pet salamander – by his bed. He was a long black lizard who had such icy cold skin that he could put out fires. 'I don't know which class I'll enter him in,' replied Storm uncertainly. 'Salamanders are lovely but they don't do very much, and there isn't likely to be a putting-out-fire class.'

Azure appeared back at the table, having overheard what they were talking about. 'You've got a salamander!' she said, looking at Storm. 'Poor you! They have to be one of the most *boring* pets in the whole world!'

'Archie isn't boring,' Storm protested.

Azure raised her eyebrows disbelievingly. 'What else can he do then?'

Willow saw Storm look embarrassed and she stepped forward. 'He can do loads of things, so there,' she told Azure hotly.

'Like what?' Azure looked scornful.

'He can change colour and run really fast and he can sing!' The words rushed out of Storm.

Willow looked at him in surprise. So did Azure.

'He can really do all that stuff?' Azure said doubtfully. When Storm nodded, Azure looked a bit put out. 'Oh. Well, I'm sure my fox will still win the prize for best in the show, even if your salamander isn't as dumb as salamanders usually are.' She cantered off.

Sapphire turned to Storm. 'You never told us Archie could do all those things,' she said quietly.

'Well, he's . . . he's a special type of salamander,' mumbled Storm.

'I can't wait to see him!' said Troy. 'Tell us all about him.'

Storm shifted uncomfortably.

'Actually, I've got a tummy-ache. I think I'll go to bed.'

'But it's really early,' protested Troy. But Storm was already trotting away.

'I hope he feels better soon,' said Sapphire in concern. She turned back to the others. 'So, what classes do you think there will be?'

For the rest of the evening the unicorns discussed their pets and what classes they would like to enter them in. When they went up to the cloud stable that evening, Willow looked over Storm's door. He was lying down, his eyes closed.

'How are you feeling?' she called softly. But Storm didn't answer.

*He must be asleep*, Willow thought. She whinnied a goodnight and then lay down on the soft cloud bed in her stable. Shutting her eyes, she imagined standing in a show ring with Whizzy being given a first-place rosette. She refused to let herself think about the fact she had lied about Whizzy's abilities. The pet show was going to be fun and nothing was going to ruin it!

# Time to Decorate

'Wake up! Wake up!'

Willow blinked her eyes open. Troy was standing outside her stall, his ears pricked.

'I was up early to practise my flying and when I flew over the Assembly Fields I saw that the pet show schedule has been put up on the Telling Tree,' Troy whinnied excitedly. 'Come and see!'

Willow, Storm and Sapphire followed Troy out of the cloud stables.

The Telling Tree stood at one end of the Assembly Fields. It was a very old tree with a thick trunk and twisted branches. The leaves on it were copper-coloured and at different times of the year different flowers grew at the end of the branches. Just then the flowers were a pale blue colour. A large piece of paper was held in place on the trunk by twigs that looked like hands. The title was written in large purple letters, with the list of classes beneath it:

## Show Schedule

Class One: Prettiest Pet

Class Two: Most Handsome Pet

Class Three: Pet with the Best
Singing Voice

Class Four: Fastest Pet

Class Five: Obstacle Course

Class Six: Most Colourful Pet

Class Seven: Pet with the Best
Trick

Class Eight: (for the winners of
all the other classes) Best Pet in
the Show

'All the classes sound fun!' said
Sapphire. 'I think I'll enter Flutter in
the Prettiest Pet.'

Willow couldn't decide between

entering Whizzy in the Prettiest Pet,
the Pet with the Best Singing Voice
or the Obstacle Course!

'I think I'll enter Jet in the Most
Handsome Pet,' said Troy. 'How
about you, Storm? What will you
take Archie in?'

'I don't know,' Storm replied
doubtfully.

Willow smiled at him. 'I bet

Archie beats Azure's magic fox and wins best in the show.'

'Mmm.' Storm cleared his throat and changed the subject. 'So, do you think we'll have to help get the school ready for the show?'

'I hope so!' said Sapphire.

To their delight, in transformation class that morning, Tor, their teacher, told them that they were going to be learning how to use their magic to transform pieces of string into streamers and banners.

'The best decorations will be used at the garden party,' he said. He touched his horn to a piece of string lying on the ground. It changed into a soft turquoise rope hung with rainbow-coloured stars.

'The choice of decoration is up to you,' Tor explained. 'Imagine what you want the decoration to look like, concentrate on it really hard and then touch your horn to the string and let your magic do the rest!'

It sounded easy but it wasn't! Willow tried again and again, but although she was imagining a beautiful purple ribbon hung with lots of paper butterflies and dragonflies, all she managed to do was get the rope to change to a dirty blue colour with a few limp pieces of paper that didn't look anything like the beautiful decoration she had been imagining.

She glanced across at Storm. He was really good at transforming things usually, but to her surprise his decoration didn't look any better than hers. The string was frayed and a few lumpy-looking paper unicorns hung from it, their ears drooping dejectedly.

Storm saw her looking and sighed. 'I don't know what's wrong. My magic just doesn't seem to be working today.'

Tor came over. 'Is there something bothering you, Storm? Often if you're worried about something it can interfere with your ability to do magic.'

'I'm fine,' Storm said quickly.

'Well, try again then,' Tor said.
'You too, Willow.'

Willow sighed to herself silently.
Storm might be fine but she still felt
a little bit guilty for lying about her
pet. She wished she hadn't fibbed.

They kept trying and Willow did
manage to transform her string into
a purple ribbon hung with ten
butterflies and dragonflies. But
Storm still didn't have any luck.

'Why couldn't you do it?' Troy
asked him as they made their way
to lunch after class.

'I don't know,' he said sadly.

Willow remembered what Tor had
said and how her guilty feelings had

made it hard to focus on her magic. 'You're absolutely sure there isn't anything bothering you?' she asked.

'I'm sure,' replied Storm, but he avoided her eyes.

'Maybe you'll feel better after lunch,' said Sapphire, who'd also had problems transforming her string into decorations. 'Things always look better on a full stomach.'

Storm nodded. But Willow noticed that he didn't seem very hungry at lunchtime and he left the table early.

Willow and the others found him in the courtyard, pacing around, deep in thought, near to the elfmail office.

He looked up as he heard their hooves. 'Oh, hi,' he muttered.

'Are you OK?' Sapphire asked him.

Storm shrugged. 'Yes.'

Willow looked at him. He didn't sound OK. 'Should we go to the mailroom and get the entry forms for the pet show?' she suggested, hoping it would cheer him up. Sapphire and Troy nodded and Willow led the way over to the big wooden door. She pushed it open. A tall elf was sitting behind a desk. On the other side of the room three more elves were sorting letters and parcels on to shelves. Oriel was in the office, reading a letter.

'Hi, Oriel,' Troy said.

'Hello,' Oriel replied unhappily.

'What's the matter?' Willow asked him.

'I came in here to fill in my entry form and found out I've got a letter from home,' Oriel answered. 'It's not good news. My mum has hurt her leg and because my dad's away there's not going to be anyone to bring my pet squirrel, Charlie, to school for the pet show.'

'Will your mum be all right?' Sapphire asked anxiously.

Oriel nodded. 'She says she'll be better in a week or so, she just needs to rest.' He sighed. 'I'm glad she's going to be OK, I just really wanted to enter Charlie in the show.'

Willow nuzzled him. 'Maybe you could borrow a pet,' she said. 'If the Tricorn says it's OK you can take Whizzy in one of the classes.'

'Or Flutter,' offered Sapphire.

'Or Jet,' put in Troy.

'Or Archie, but he's not very good with other people,' said Storm in a quiet voice.

'That's really nice of you all.' Oriel looked round at them. 'But it wouldn't really be the same. Still, perhaps I should go and ask the Tricorn if I can anyway.'

While they waited for him to come back, they filled in their entry forms. Willow decided to enter Whizzy for the Obstacle Course in the end because it sounded most fun. She glanced at Storm. He was staring at the mailboxes with a thoughtful look on his face. She poked him with her horn. 'Hey, you haven't filled in your form yet!'

He jumped. 'Oh! Sorry, I was miles away.'

Sapphire grinned at him. 'It must be hard to choose which class to go in when you've got a pet as clever as Archie!'

'Yes, what *are* you going to enter him in?' Troy asked Storm.

Storm glanced down at Willow's form. 'I think I'll go in the Obstacle Course too,' he said, quickly filling in his form.

They had just put their entry forms into the box when Oriel came trotting back into the office.

'What did the Tricorn say?' Storm asked him eagerly.

'He says I can't borrow a pet,' said

Oriel. 'The rule is one entry per pet and it has to be a pet you've trained and looked after. But he did say that seeing as I couldn't enter, I could be a steward. That means I get to call unicorns in for the classes and help give out the prizes. It'll be almost as much fun as going in the show!'

Willow was delighted to see Oriel looking happier.

'Thanks for offering me your pets though,' Oriel said. 'You're really good friends! I'm going to tell everyone else I'm going to be a steward.'

As Oriel left the office, Storm pricked up his ears. 'Being a steward would be great! Um, I'm just going

to do something. I'll see you later!'
he said, trotting away.

As Storm disappeared, Willow
turned to her friends. 'He's behaving
very strangely today, you know,' she
said, staring after him.

'He is being a bit odd,' agreed
Sapphire.

'He says there's nothing wrong
though,' put in Troy.

'I guess,' said Willow, but she wasn't convinced. Something *was* bothering Storm. She was sure of it.

Willow, Sapphire and Troy didn't get to see Storm again until lunchtime was almost over. They were just about to go to the Flying Heath for their first lesson after lunch when Willow spotted him coming out of the elfmail office. 'There he is!' she called.

They cantered over, just as the horn for the end of lunchtime rang.

'Oh, hi,' Storm said happily. His ears were pricked and there was a spring in his step.

'Have you been posting a letter?' Sapphire asked him.

'No,' Storm said. 'I . . . I just got a letter.' He looked suddenly sad. 'It was from my mum. Archie's ill so he's not going to be able to come to the pet show after all.'

'Oh no!' gasped Willow. 'What's the matter with him?'

'He's got a temperature,' said Storm. 'He's really sick.'

'But that's awful,' Troy said.

Storm nodded sadly. 'I was really hoping I could enter him in the show. But there's no way he'll be better in time.'

'Oh, Storm.' Willow nuzzled him. 'Look, maybe the Tricorn will let you be a steward like Oriel.'

'I'll go and ask when lessons are

over!' Storm tossed his head excitedly. 'Being a steward will be loads of fun!' he said, flying upwards.

As Willow followed him, she felt a bit surprised that he didn't seem more upset. Of course being a steward would be exciting, but Archie was ill.

As she flew after him she noticed two spots of purple ink on Storm's front legs. 'Have you been writing a letter?' she called over to him.

Storm looked guilty. 'No. Why?'

'You've got ink on your legs,' Willow pointed out.

'I was doodling on some paper earlier,' Storm said. 'I must have splashed myself with ink then.'

'You know, it's odd you got a letter from your parents at lunchtime.' Troy drew up alongside them. 'The elves only deliver mail in the mornings and evenings.'

'I . . . I was just passing the office and one of the elves called me in,' said Storm.

Willow blinked. 'They don't usually do that.'

'I guess it was because it was an urgent letter,' Storm said quickly. He speeded up. 'Come on! We don't want to be late for our flying class!'

# What's the Matter
# with Storm?

The next few days rushed by.
While the older unicorns
magicked delicious food, and
transformed the trees so they were
all different colours, the Year Ones
kept practising making decorations.
By the end of the week, Willow had
managed to make two beautiful

ribbons of multi-
coloured butterflies and dragonflies.
Storm had made ten different
banners. He was back to
being the best at
transformation in the year. And
back to being his usual cheerful
self.
Willow couldn't help
thinking it was a bit odd.
Whenever she asked him
about Archie, all that Storm
said was that he was still ill,

but he didn't seem worried about him at all.

'I can't wait until the pets arrive tomorrow,' Troy said as they got up on Friday.

'I really want to meet Whizzy, Jet and Flutter,' said Storm.

'Yeah, I want to see Whizzy fly so fast she turns invisible,' said Troy. 'And watch Flutter make flowers change colour.'

Willow felt uncomfortable. She'd been hoping the others might have forgotten what she'd said about Whizzy. 'It might be too crowded for Whizzy to fly really fast,' she said quickly.

'And Flutter is quite shy, she

doesn't like changing the colour of flowers in front of people,' said Sapphire.

'Well, I hope Azure doesn't win Best Pet in the Show then,' Troy said. 'She's been boasting all week about how amazing her magic fox is and how he is definitely going to win.'

'Is Archie getting any better, Storm?' Sapphire asked.

'I haven't heard from Mum and Dad for a couple of days, but I suppose no news is good news,' Storm said cheerfully.

Willow walked out of her stable. 'Oh, there's a letter for you!' she said, seeing an envelope outside

Storm's stall. She picked it up in her mouth and passed it over the door.

'Thanks,' said Storm, opening it up.

Willow heard him catch his breath. She glanced over the door. He was looking dismayed. 'What's the matter?'

'Nothing.' Storm gulped.

'Is it from your mum and dad?' Sapphire asked.

Storm nodded. He crumpled the letter up and shoved it under his bed.

'Do they say how Archie is?' asked Willow.

'Y-yes,' Storm stammered. 'He's getting better and he's going to be able to come to the show after all.'

'But that's great!' said Troy.

'I guess it is,' Storm mumbled. 'I'm going down for breakfast.'

He came out of his stable and set off at a trot. Willow stared after him. Surely if Archie was able to come to the show, then Storm should be delighted? But he looked really upset! *What's going on?* she thought. *I'll talk to him after breakfast*, she decided.

But Storm went off to talk to Tor after breakfast and didn't meet up with the others until their first lesson started. As it ended, Willow went over to him. 'Storm?'

'Yes,' he said.

'Are you OK? You don't seem very happy that Archie is better.'

'Of course I am!' Storm said.

'But . . .'

'Um, look, I've got to go!' Storm interrupted. 'I promised to help Tor with the decorating this break time – and lunchtime too. See you!'

Willow stared after Storm as he cantered away. She had the distinct feeling he had wanted to avoid talking to her. He didn't come anywhere near her for the rest of the day.

'Storm's behaving really strangely,' Willow said to Sapphire as they began to graze after supper – Troy had gone off to talk to Atlas, the flying teacher, and Storm had disappeared again. 'Have you noticed?'

'No, not really.' Sapphire sounded distracted.

Willow looked at her and suddenly realized that Sapphire had been very quiet all day too. 'Are you OK?' she asked, wondering what the matter was with all her friends.

Sapphire hesitated and then sighed. 'No, I'm not.'

'What's up?' Willow asked.

Sapphire looked really anxious. 'It's the pet show. Oh, Willow.' The words tumbled out of Sapphire. 'I feel awful and I don't know what to do. You know I said that Flutter could make flowers change colour?' Willow nodded. Sapphire looked shame-faced. 'Well, she can't. I lied. I don't know why; it was just that Oriel was teasing me about Flutter not doing anything but looking pretty and the words popped out.'

Willow felt a rush of relief. 'Oh, Sapphire, I did the same thing! Whizzy can't fly so fast that he looks invisible. I just said it because everyone else's pets seemed to be able to do these amazing things.'

Sapphire stared at her. 'So we both made things up?'

Willow nodded. 'I've been feeling guilty about it too.'

Sapphire nuzzled Willow's nose. 'We've been really silly, haven't we?'

'Yes,' Willow agreed. 'I suppose we're going to have to tell the others.'

'At least we can do it together,' Sapphire told her.

Willow felt much better at the thought.

'So why are you worried about Storm?' Sapphire asked.

'I don't know. It's just that I thought he would have been happier that Archie was better.'

'You're right,' said Sapphire thoughtfully. 'Let's go and find him.'

Willow and Sapphire cantered off and began to hunt round for Storm. They couldn't see him in the meadows, but finally they found him in the cloud stable. To their surprise they saw that he was packing a bag with his things. 'What are you doing?' Willow asked in surprise.

Storm jumped. 'Nothing!' He guiltily kicked the bag under his cloud bed. 'I'm just sorting some stuff out.'

'Are you OK, Storm?' Sapphire asked. 'You don't seem very pleased that Archie can come to the show.'

'Of course I am!' Storm protested.

'Oh, look, I've just remembered, Tor wants me to do something.'

'Storm!' exclaimed Willow. From the look on Storm's face she was sure he had been making it up about Tor, but Storm had already cantered off.

'He keeps doing that!' Willow exclaimed in exasperation.

'You're right. He *is* acting weird,' said Sapphire. 'Let's wait here and talk to him when he comes back.'

But Storm didn't come back until
the elves were blowing the horns
for the unicorns to go to sleep.
Then he went straight into his stable
and put his head down.

'Night,' Willow called to him,
deciding she would speak to him in
the morning.

He didn't reply.

When Willow blinked her eyes open
the next morning, she thought
about the pet show and jumped to
her feet. It was the big day. Their
parents would be arriving at
lunchtime with their pets! She
couldn't wait to see Whizzy again.

'Wake up, Sapphire!' she whinnied.

'Wake up, Storm! Wake up, everyone! It's the pet show!'

She heard Sapphire and Troy whinny and start to get to their feet. Willow went over to the partition between her and Storm's stalls. 'Are you awake, Storm —' She broke off as she looked over the partition. Storm's stall was empty.

*That's strange*, Willow thought. She looked around the stall and her eyes widened. Everything had gone — his bag, the photos he had of Archie and of his parents, his blue stable blanket for cold nights, his collection of plants and leaves that he used when he was transforming things. A cold feeling swept over Willow.

There was only one explanation for Storm and all his things not being there. He must have run away!

# Chapter Five

# Missing!

'What do you mean Storm's run away?' Sapphire gasped a few minutes later.

'He must have done. All of his things have gone!' said Willow, going into Storm's stall. Sapphire and Troy watched from the doorway.

'Do you remember seeing him

packing his things into his bag yesterday?' Willow said to Sapphire. 'Maybe he was planning all along to get up early and go.'

'But why?' demanded Sapphire.

'It doesn't make sense,' said Troy. 'It's the pet show today. Why would he want to miss that? Particularly now Archie's better.'

They all looked at each other, puzzled. Why *would* Storm run away?

'What's that beside his bed?' said Sapphire suddenly, pointing to a crumpled piece of paper.

'It's a letter,' Willow said, picking it up. 'Maybe it's from Storm telling us where he's gone.'

'Read it!' Troy urged. 'If we know where he is then we can go after him and make him come back!'

Willow's eyes skimmed over the first lines.

*Dear Storm,*
*We got your letter saying that the pet show had been cancelled . . .*

Her eyes jumped to the end of the letter:

*Lots of love, Mum and Dad xxx*

'It's not from Storm,' she said, looking up. 'It's a letter *to* him from his mum and dad. It's probably the one he got yesterday −' She broke off suddenly as she realized what the letter had said. She re-read the first sentence:

*We got your letter saying that the pet show had been cancelled . . .*

But that didn't make sense. The pet show hadn't been cancelled! Why had Storm sent his parents a letter saying that it had?

'What's the matter?' Sapphire asked, looking at Willow's puzzled face.

'It's just something this letter says.' Willow hesitated. It was Storm's private letter from his parents and she didn't feel like she should really read it. But it was odd and maybe if she read it, it would help them work out what the matter was with him and why he had run away.

*Dear Storm,*

*We got your letter saying that the pet show had been cancelled. But we were speaking to Topaz's parents yesterday and they told us that the pet show was still on. There's obviously been some mix-up! Anyway, don't worry. We'll be there on Saturday with Archie. He's very well but missing you. See you on Saturday!*

*Lots of love, Mum and Dad xxx*

'This is really weird,' said Willow. 'Storm seems to have told his parents that the show was cancelled, but the letter says they've found out that it isn't. It doesn't mention anything about Archie being ill. In fact, it says that he's missing Storm but is very well!'

Troy stared. 'But that doesn't make any sense.'

'I know,' Willow said. 'Why would Storm lie to us and say Archie's ill and lie to his parents and tell them the pet show's off?'

'Unless he didn't want Archie to come to the show,' Sapphire said slowly. She looked at Willow. 'You don't think Storm could have been doing what we did? Saying things about Archie that weren't true?'

Willow's eyes widened. 'You mean maybe he might have been making it up about Archie being a special type of salamander?'

Sapphire nodded.

'What are you two going on about?' Troy said, looking mystified.

Willow bit her lip. 'Sapphire and I didn't quite tell the truth about Flutter and Whizzy. Flutter can't make flowers change colour and Whizzy can't fly so fast she goes invisible.'

'We just said it because your pet – and Oriel's and Azure's – sounded so amazing,' said Sapphire.

'You lied?' Troy said, looking surprised.

Willow looked at him. 'Yes and we shouldn't have done it, but it's not always easy to tell the truth, is it, Troy?'

Their eyes met. Troy looked suddenly uncomfortable and Willow was sure he was remembering a time when he had lied to them by not telling them the truth that he was a prince.

'I guess not,' he sighed, the indignation leaving his face.

'If Storm had been making it up that Archie could do lots of amazing things he would have known we would find out the truth at the pet show,' Willow said.

'So maybe that's why he told his parents that the show was cancelled because then they wouldn't come,' Sapphire joined in.

Willow nodded. 'But then he got this letter yesterday and realized his parents were going to bring Archie to the show after all . . .'

'And he knew then that we'd find out he hadn't been telling the truth,' broke in Troy. 'So he decided to run away.'

They all stared at each other.

'Oh, poor Storm,' Sapphire said. 'He must have been feeling awful.'

'We *have* to go after him!' declared Willow.

'Maybe we should tell a teacher,' said Sapphire worriedly.

'But then Storm will get into loads of trouble for running away,' said Willow. 'If we can get him to come back to school before the show starts, no one will ever know.'

'Willow's right,' Troy said to Sapphire. 'We don't want Storm to get into trouble. Let's try and find him ourselves.'

Sapphire nodded. 'All right. But how are we going to find him? We don't know where he's gone.'

'We could use rose quartz,' suggested Willow, thinking of the power whereby unicorns could touch their horns to rose quartz and see where anyone in the world was. 'Let's go to the Rose Quartz Cliffs.'

They raced out of the stables. The other unicorns were all heading towards the meadows for breakfast, but Willow, Sapphire and Troy flew east towards the white sandy beach and pinky-grey Rose Quartz Cliffs.

They landed on the soft sand. Sapphire, who was the best out of the three of them at rose-quartz gazing, lowered her head until her horn was touching one of the rocks in the cliff. 'Show me Storm,' she said.

There was a bright purple flash and a mist swirled. As it cleared, the surface of the rock began to shine like a mirror. A picture formed in it. Willow stepped forward eagerly. 'There's Storm!' she said, seeing their friend trudging towards a mountain, his bag round his neck. He looked very dejected, his ears were drooping and his head hung low.

'Where is he?' said Willow, looking at the countryside in the picture.

'He's near a mountain,' Sapphire pointed out.

'It's the Misty Mountain,' Troy said. 'I've been there with my father. It's not too far away from here. It's very dangerous because a mist can come down at any moment. My dad says when that happens it's really easy to get lost or walk over a cliff edge!'

Willow felt very alarmed. What if Storm didn't know that? 'We have to go and find Storm and bring him back!'

'But we're not really meant to go beyond the school boundaries,' said Sapphire in a quiet little voice.

'But he could be in danger!' said Troy. 'Finding Storm is more important than keeping to the rules.'

'You're right,' Sapphire nodded. And with that, the three friends flew into the air.

'Come on! Let's go!'

## Chapter
## Six

# Lost in the Mist

As Willow, Sapphire and Troy flew out over the school boundaries, Willow's heart beat hard. How must Storm be feeling? It must be horrible for him being away from school and all alone.

They swooped over a thick forest and across some wide grassy fields criss-crossed by sparkling streams, with Troy leading the way. In the distance, a craggy, thickly wooded mountain loomed up. 'That's the Misty Mountain!' he called over his shoulder.

As they reached the lower slopes, they landed beside a river that disappeared into some dark trees. A mist was swirling over the top half

of the mountain. Willow shivered in
alarm. She had no idea what sort of
creatures lived on Misty Mountain,
but it looked like the sort of place
where there might be trolls and
monsters.

Sapphire looked around uneasily. 'I
hope we find Storm quickly. I don't
like it here.'

'Me neither,' said Willow. 'Let's try
and find some rose quartz and see if

we can find out where on the mountain Storm is.'

They all hunted around. Troy finally found a pinky-grey rock, half hidden by a layer of moss. 'Here!' he said, scraping the moss off with his hoof. 'Quick, Sapphire!'

Sapphire trotted over and murmured Storm's name. As the picture appeared in the rock's surface, Willow saw that Storm was standing among some trees, near a waterfall and a river. He looked very miserable. 'There he is!' she cried.

'But how are we going to find him?' said Sapphire.

'This river might lead to the waterfall,' Willow said hopefully. 'If we follow it then we might find Storm.'

'Good idea!' said Troy as they walked into the trees.

It was murky and there were lots of shadows. Willow was sure she could feel eyes looking at her from behind bushes and tree trunks. As they got further and further into the woods, the leaves overhead cut out the light and the murkiness thickened. The three friends slowed down. They could just see beyond the end of their noses. Troy stumbled over a tree root and Willow jumped as a branch caught at her coat.

'I can hardly see a thing,' said Troy, peering through the gloom.

'I . . . I'm scared,' Sapphire whispered.

Willow could hear the tremble in her friend's voice. She fought down her own fear and nuzzled Sapphire's neck. 'Don't worry. It'll be fine.'

'I wish we had magic that would let us see in the dark. It's going to take us ages to get to Storm,' Troy said.

'We've just got to keep walking!' Willow said, pushing past them both and heading determinedly up the hill. They couldn't let the murkiness put them off. Surely if they just kept close to the river they would find the waterfall and hopefully find Storm.

Willow marched onwards. There were strange rustles in the bushes nearby and every so often a bird would screech in the branches overhead making Willow jump. Suddenly she heard something that made her stop dead. Something big seemed to be coming down the hill towards them! It was crashing through the bushes and the undergrowth.

Sapphire and Troy froze too.

'W-what's that?' Sapphire stammered.

'I don't know but it sounds really big!' said Troy.

Willow gulped and edged back down the track slightly. What should they do? It could be a troll or an ogre or . . . or . . .

'Ow!' the thing coming towards them exclaimed.

'Storm!' Willow, Sapphire and Troy cried together.

The crashing stopped. There was silence. 'Willow? Sapphire? Troy?' Storm's voice echoed through the still air.

'Yes! It's us!' Willow whinnied. She cantered forward. 'Storm! Where are you? Where . . .' She broke off as she bumped noses with him. 'Oh, Storm!' she whinnied joyfully, nuzzling him. 'We've found you!'

The other two joined them. 'We

thought you were a monster!'
exclaimed Sapphire.

'What are you all doing here?'
Storm said, astonished. His eyes were
large in the gloom.

'We came to find you,' said Troy,
pushing him with his nose. 'We
were worried about you.'

'I'm so glad you're here,' said Storm in relief. 'I thought I was lost!'

'Why did you run away?' Willow demanded.

'Was it because of Archie?' said Sapphire softly.

'No, it was . . .' Storm spoke quickly, but then he broke off and hung his head. 'Yes, you're right. It *was* because of Archie. He isn't a super-special salamander. I made it up. I'm really, really sorry,' he said in a rush. 'I know it was wrong and I shouldn't have done it.'

'Oh, Storm, don't feel bad,' said Sapphire. 'Willow and I made up stuff about Flutter and Whizzy too.'

'Whizzy can't fly so fast she turns

invisible and Flutter can't change the colour of flowers,' Willow said.

'Really?' said Storm. They whinnied in agreement and Storm gave a sigh of relief. 'I've been feeling so awful about lying and about being ashamed of Archie. Even if he can't do special things I love him and I know I shouldn't have felt embarrassed by him. I lied to my parents too. I . . . I told them that the pet show was cancelled so they wouldn't bring Archie.'

'We know,' Willow told him. 'You dropped the letter your parents sent you, Storm. I wouldn't have read it, but we were so worried about you. We know what you told your parents and we know that Archie wasn't really ill.'

'It doesn't matter though,' said Troy quickly. 'We just want you to come back to school.'

'But what about the pet show?' Storm said. 'I know Archie's not the most beautiful pet in the world and he can't do anything clever, but I really do love him and I don't want people to laugh at him in case it upsets him.'

'Well, we won't laugh at him,' declared Willow.

'What about Azure?' said Storm.

'Don't worry about her,' said Troy. 'She's probably been making things up about her silly fox too! And even if she hasn't, we'll be there with you and we won't let her tease you.'

Willow nuzzled his neck. 'I really want to meet Archie. He might not do clever tricks but he must be pretty special if you love him as much as you do.'

'And I bet our pets will love him too,' said Sapphire. 'You *have* to come back with us, Storm.'

Storm looked round at them. 'All right, I will.' He breathed out a big sigh. 'I'm so lucky you're my friends.'

Willow grinned. 'We're lucky you're our friend too. Even if you did scare us half to death coming down the mountain and sounding like a monster! Come on, let's get back to school.'

'Hang on! Look at the mist!' said Troy suddenly.

They looked up. A silvery-grey mist was swirling down the mountain through the trees towards them. It rushed over their bodies and covered them up. Willow couldn't even see the others. 'Troy? Sapphire? Storm?' she cried.

'I can't see a thing,' came Sapphire's voice through the mist.

'Neither can I!' said Troy.

'The mist is really thick,' said Willow, looking round. 'I think this might be the way.'

She took a few cautious steps

forward and then felt her hooves
sliding on rock. She gasped and
jumped back, only just in time to
stop herself slipping into the river.
'No, it's not!' she said, lowering her
head and spotting the wet rocks with
clusters of flowers growing between
them. 'This way is the river!'

'We're never going to find our way back in time for the pet show,' said Sapphire in dismay.

'This is all my fault!' said Storm. 'We wouldn't be stuck here if it wasn't for me.'

'If only there was some magic we could use . . .' Willow had an idea. 'I know! What about the clearing fog magic that we've been learning in weather classes?'

'Of course!' said Troy. 'A mist is just like a fog.'

'But we'll need a moonflower,' said Sapphire.

'I think I saw some just now when my hooves slipped on the rocks!' said Willow. She took a cautious step forward and lowered her head. She could just about see the rocks she had stepped on. Moonflowers were growing between them. 'Here!' she said triumphantly as she pulled a flower up. 'What we need to do is try and make a tunnel in the mist so we can see our way out through the trees and down the mountain. One, two, three!' She threw the flower into the air and quickly circled round it with her horn. As the flower fell to the floor, a tunnel of clear air appeared in the mist. Through it Willow could see the path leading down through the trees beside the river.

'It's working!' she whinnied.
'Come on!'

They all galloped down the tunnel and burst out of the mist at the bottom of the mountain. The warm sun shone down on their backs and Willow gave a buck of delight. 'We're not lost any more!'

Troy plunged into the sky. 'Let's just hope we can get back to school in time!'

# Chapter Seven

# The Pet Show

Willow and the others galloped over the fields and woods. Just as they flew over the school boundaries, they heard an announcement ringing out. 'The pet show will begin in twenty minutes. Will any pupils who haven't collected their pets from their parents please do so now.'

'We've made it!' exclaimed Troy.

'We'd better find our parents!' panted Sapphire.

The school looked amazing – banners and streamers hung from the trees and a pet show arena had been marked out in the Assembly Fields with rainbow-coloured ribbon. There was a silver table with the rosettes on and a shining trophy for the best pet in the show. There were unicorns and pets everywhere!

'Mum! Dad!' whinnied Willow, spotting two unicorns with a tiny red-and-gold hummingbird flying around their heads. She landed beside them.

Her dad smiled at her. 'There you are, Willow! We were wondering what had happened to you.'

'Hello, sweetheart,' her mum said. 'It's lovely to see you.'

'And you,' Willow said joyfully. Her hummingbird landed on her horn and chirruped loudly. 'Hi, Whizzy,' Willow grinned. 'Have you missed me?'

The little bird pushed the side of his head against her face in reply.

Willow looked around. Lots of the unicorns seemed to have rabbits and mice but there were others with more unusual pets. Juniper had a bright blue dragonfly, Cloud had a prancing deer and Topaz had a baby phoenix. And there was Azure! She was proudly leading her fox. He had a rich red coat with white stripes down his back and his dark eyes were sharp as they darted around. As Willow watched, he tried to shake the collar off over his head and when that failed he began to change shape! First he changed into a dog and then a cat. Azure struggled to hold on to the lead as the fox twisted and turned.

'Azure! Please make sure you keep your pet under control!' the Tricorn called from the platform at the end of the Assembly Fields. 'Magic foxes can be very tricky creatures.'

Looking at his concerned face, Willow had the impression that the Tricorn wasn't very pleased to have a magic fox in the school grounds.

Troy was standing beside the platform with his mother, a noble snow-white unicorn with a circlet of shining jewels around her horn. A sleek black panther with green eyes and a white circle of hairs on his back sat quietly beside Troy, his tail curled neatly round his paws.

Sapphire was nearby with her mum, dad and three of her younger brothers and sisters. There was a large pink-and-purple butterfly fluttering around her ears.

'I'm just going to take Whizzy over to see Sapphire and Troy,' Willow told her parents.

'OK. We'll go and find somewhere around the ringside to watch the show from,' her dad replied. 'Which class are you in?'

'Class Five – the Obstacle Course,' Willow answered.

'Good luck! We'll see you after it!' her mum said.

'Thanks.' Willow touched noses with her parents and headed off with Whizzy.

Troy had joined Sapphire and her family. Willow whinnied. 'This is Whizzy!'

'He's so cute!' Sapphire exclaimed as the hummingbird zoomed in a circle round Willow's horn before perching between Willow's ears and chirruping loudly.

'Your pets are lovely too,' Willow said, looking at Jet and Flutter.

Storm came over. He had a blue blanket over his back and sitting on it was a large black salamander with red spots.

'Is that Archie? He's beautiful,'

Willow said. It wasn't *exactly* true.
Archie's black coat was going grey
around his legs and his scales looked
dull. But his eyes shone like bright
dark jewels.

'I love his red spots,' said Troy.

'And his eyes are amazing,' said
Sapphire.

Storm looked very pleased. Willow

stepped forward to nuzzle Archie. 'Oh, don't touch him!' Storm said quickly.

'Why not?' Willow was surprised.

'Because his skin is so cold. If you touch him you'll get frostbite. That's why he has to sit on a blanket on my back. All salamanders are like that. It means they can live in fires and put them out if they want to.'

There was a crackle from a loudspeaker nearby and then Atlas made an announcement.

'Would all the contestants for Class One – the Prettiest Pet – please bring their pets into the ring.'

'That's me!' Sapphire said excitedly. 'I'm taking Flutter in that class!'

'Good luck!' the other three whinnied.

Sapphire trotted towards the ring with Flutter flying beside her. Oriel was standing at the entrance with a red sash round his neck that said 'Ring Steward' in big silver letters. He checked everyone's names against a big board and then let them into the ring. They all had to line up around the edge and then the show started!

There were three judges – the Tricorn, Tor and Damaris, the charms teacher. They walked around and had a good look at all the pets. Cloud's deer was chosen as the winner, a striped squirrel was second and, to Willow's delight, Sapphire came third with Flutter. She came out of the ring with a big yellow rosette.

'Well done!' the others neighed.

'Thank you!' Sapphire looked thrilled.

'Would all contestants for Class Two please come into the ring!' Atlas called.

'This is my class,' Troy said.

Jet was easily the most hand-some pet in the ring and he was very well-behaved. He purred at the judges and didn't move a muscle when they were looking at him. Troy had trained him very well.

The judges gave Troy the red rosette. 'He's won!' exclaimed Willow.

'That means he can go in the Best in the Show class at the end of the day,' said Storm.

As Troy came out to the sound of loud cheers, Azure was passing the ring entrance. 'Of course, my fox would have won that class easily!' she declared. 'He's much more handsome than Troy's panther. It's such a shame we are only allowed to enter one class.'

Willow, Sapphire and Storm trotted over to congratulate Troy. He was delighted to have won. 'I hope one of you wins the Obstacle

Course,' he said to Willow and Storm.

Willow felt excitement bubble in her tummy. Now she'd watched the first two classes, she couldn't wait for her turn!

Class Three – the Pet with the Best Singing Voice – was won by a Year Four unicorn called Rose with her beautiful grey lovebird, and Class Four – the Fastest Pet – was won by Juniper's dragonfly. At last it was time for the Obstacle Course.

The course was put out in the ring. The pets had to weave in and out of poles, go under and over jumps, over a bridge, through a tunnel, go round a stick with ribbons tied on it three times, and then they had to race across the finish line. The pet who did everything and who was the fastest would be the winner. There were twelve pets entered. Willow was fifth in the ring. As she walked through the entrance with Whizzy flying beside her she felt as if she had a butterfly as big as Flutter in her stomach!

She and Whizzy waited at the start. A hush fell and then Oriel blew a whistle and they were off! Willow galloped as fast as she could round the course, with Whizzy zipping along beside her going over the jumps and through the poles. The little bird did everything perfectly

and they finished
with the fastest time
in the competition so
far.

'Well done, Whizzy!'
Willow gasped as they
left the ring.

The hummingbird
sang happily.

'That was brilliant, Willow!'
Storm exclaimed. 'You were really
fast!'

'Thanks. Good luck!' she said,
joining Sapphire and Troy. 'I hope
Storm does well,' she said to them.

But Storm didn't. Archie strolled
around and wouldn't speed up,
despite Storm urging him to. He

seemed to get slower and slower and then made everyone laugh when he reached the bridge and lay down, shut his eyes and refused to move.

'Come on, Archie!' Storm urged.

Archie just opened one eye and stared at him.

'Oh, poor Storm,' said Willow.

'It's OK, Willow. He doesn't look too upset,' said Sapphire.

Willow looked at Storm's face and saw that he was grinning.

He bent his head close to the salamander's. 'Please?' he said hopefully.

Archie sighed, got to his feet and walked on to the bridge. The audience cheered. Archie waddled three times round the pole before marching over the finishing line and stopping to take a big mouthful of grass. He munched it happily, long strands hanging from his mouth.

'Well, that was the slowest round yet,' Atlas announced. 'But well done Storm and Archie for not giving up and for finishing the course.'

Everyone cheered again.

Archie looked up at the audience

and nodded his head as if bowing to them.

'He's brilliant!' Troy laughed. 'The audience love him. He's definitely the funniest pet!'

'He's the most *stupid* one,' a voice sneered beside them. They looked round and saw Azure there with her fox who was pulling at his lead.

'Archie isn't stupid!' Willow said hotly.

'I think Storm's lucky to have him,' Sapphire said.

'Me too,' put in Troy. 'Archie's great.'

'Well, I'm very glad I don't have a rubbish pet like that,' Azure said. 'I'd be really embarrassed.'

To Willow's horror, Storm came out of the ring at that very moment. She thought he'd be really upset, but he just turned his back on Azure. 'That was really good fun!' he said. 'I know Archie was slow, but the audience gave us a huge cheer at the end!'

'I think you did brilliantly,' Willow told him. 'And you, Archie,' she said, turning to blow at the salamander on the ground. 'You were great!'

Azure snorted scornfully, but just then her fox turned himself invisible!

Azure gave a loud squeal of horror as she looked down at the empty collar. 'Felix has gone! He's escaped!' Felix the fox reappeared and

grinned cheekily at her as if to say
'just joking'!

The others burst out laughing and
Azure looked very embarrassed.
'Come on, Felix. It's almost time
for our class,' she said crossly as she
pulled him away.

Felix looked over his shoulder and
gave Willow and her friends a wink.

'He looks really naughty,'
commented Sapphire.

Willow nodded. It would be
amazing to have a magic fox like
Felix for a pet but he did look very
difficult to control. She had the
feeling that when he was around,
anything might happen!

The show continued. Sage, a Year

Four unicorn, just beat Willow and Whizzy's time on the Obstacle Course with his pet hawk, but Willow still got a blue rosette for coming second. She was delighted. They watched a Year Two unicorn called Meadowflax win the Most Colourful Pet class with a rainbow-coloured butterfly and then it was time for Class Seven – Pet with the Best Trick.

Azure and Felix came into the ring. Felix behaved well, although his tail waved from side to side the whole time as if he wasn't happy and Azure had to keep a tight hold of his lead. But he did as she asked – he changed colour from red to blue, he vanished and reappeared, and then he changed from a fox into a unicorn and back again. No one else's pet could do anything like it and Azure was delighted when she was presented with the red rosette and she cantered out of the ring whinnying, 'I won! I won!'

'Show off!' muttered Troy.

Willow suddenly realized something. 'There's only one class left now and it's the class for Best in the Show.'

'You're in this one, Troy, because you won Class Two,' said Storm.

The loudspeaker crackled. 'Would the winners of the first seven classes please come into the ring and then the judges will decide which pet will win the trophy for Best Pet in the Show.'

'Good luck!' Sapphire called to Troy.

'I hope you beat Azure,' Willow said.

Troy took a deep breath. 'Come on, Jet,' he said, and he and his panther walked into the ring.

# Chapter Eight

# Best in the Show

As the seven pets were taken into the ring for the Best in the Show class, the watching unicorns stamped their hooves eagerly.

'I really hope Troy wins,' Willow said as the unicorns lined their pets up for the judges.

'Look at Felix!' Sapphire said.

The magic fox looked like he had
had enough of being in the ring.
He was shaking his head and trying
to scrape his collar off on the floor.
'Stand up, Felix!' Azure said tugging
on the lead, but he ignored her. He

reached round with his front paw and tried to pull his collar off. 'Stop it!' Azure exclaimed as the judges approached them. She pulled hard at the lead.

'Don't do that, Azure!' a worried-looking unicorn called from the entrance as Felix ran backwards.

'That's Azure's brother,' said Sapphire.

'Go away, Axel!' snapped Azure, pulling at Felix again.

'If you pull him he'll get upset and escape!' Axel told her.

Felix began to growl and started to change shape rapidly from a fox to a cat to a dog. Axel started to come across the ring.

'Go away!' Azure repeated, struggling to hold on to Felix.

'No. He's not happy,' Axel said, breaking into a trot. 'I told you that you shouldn't borrow him for the show. You're not old enough to handle a magic fox! You should have brought your own mouse and not borrowed *my* pet.'

Willow swung round to Sapphire and Storm. 'Did you hear that? So he's not even Azure's own pet! She borrowed him!'

Axel reached Azure. 'Steady, Felix.' He grabbed hold of his pet's lead, but it was too late. At the same moment, while changing to a cat, Felix managed to get his collar off!

Free at last, he turned back into a fox and raced across the show ring. The judges whinnied in alarm. The other pets in the ring, all apart from Jet, started to get very excited and dash around their owners. The air was filled with snorts and whinnies and neighs.

'Come here!' Azure called, cantering after Felix.

But Felix didn't. He jumped into the air, turned a somersault and disappeared!

'Catch that fox!' the Tricorn's voice boomed out.

The watching unicorns spun round in circles, but no one knew where Felix was.

Suddenly, a fire exploded by the prize table. 'He must be over there!' Willow exclaimed.

Felix reappeared beside the table. He banged his tail hard on the ground. Another fire started, the red and orange flames flickering upwards.

'Azure!' bellowed the Tricorn. 'Get

that fox under control!' Dancing
round the table, Felix banged his tail
on the ground again and again, his
eyes gleaming mischievously as a
new fire started every time.

The flames caught the covering on
the table and there was a whooshing
noise as the whole tablecloth went
up in smoke. The nearby unicorns
whinnied and ducked as bits of
burning cloth spat through the
air. Willow's heart beat faster.
Someone had to stop Felix!
  But who?
    Suddenly, a red-and-
    black salamander streaked
      across the grass and

jumped on to the burning table. The flames died as they came into contact with his icy cold body.

'It's Archie! He's put the fire out!' cried Willow.

'Go on, Archie! Do the other fires too!' whinnied Storm, cantering forwards.

Storm's salamander needed no more urging. Archie jumped from the table and on to the grass. Reaching one fire after another, he leapt on top of them and the flames sizzled out.

Then Archie turned to charge straight at Felix. Felix swung round to run away from him and ran slap-bang into Axel who was waiting with his collar and lead. The older

unicorn dropped the collar deftly
over the magic fox's head. 'Got you!'
he whinnied.

Felix sat down and looked at Axel.
Then he grinned a foxy grin. He
seemed to accept that his game was
over.

The Tricorn came over with Azure
just behind him. 'I think you had
better take Felix out of the ring,
Axel,' he said.

'But what about the Best in the Show class?' Azure protested.

The Tricorn gave her a stern look. 'The rules clearly said that unicorns must take their *own* pets into the show, Azure. If Felix belongs to your brother, then you have broken the rules and so you are disqualified. You must leave the ring *now*!'

Azure hung her head and walked out.

Willow glanced at her. Even though Azure had been really annoying, she couldn't help feeling a bit sorry for her. It would have been really horrible to have been sent out of the ring like that in front of everyone.

'Are you OK?' Willow asked.

'I feel really stupid,' Azure said in a small voice. 'I wish I hadn't borrowed Felix. I just really wanted to win and I didn't think my own mouse, Minnie, would.'

'Don't worry,' said Willow kindly, as Storm came back with Archie.

Azure lifted her head. 'I'm sorry I was so mean, Storm. Archie isn't boring or stupid. He's brilliant. If he hadn't put the fires out like that one of us might have got hurt.' She reached her nose out towards the salamander. 'Thanks, Archie.'

The salamander looked very pleased.

'Look, the class has started again!' Sapphire said suddenly. 'The judges are making their decision!'

The three judges looked at the remaining six pets in the ring and then had a quick discussion and walked up to Troy and Jet. 'Best in the Show goes to Jet, the mountain panther,' announced the Tricorn. 'Not only is he handsome, but he is obedient and well-trained too.

He was the only one of the winners who listened to his owner and stayed where he was during the unfortunate fire-lighting incident. Well done, Troy and Jet!'

Willow, Sapphire and Storm cheered more loudly than anyone as Oriel brought the big silver cup over and the Tricorn presented it to Troy. Then he raised his horn and silence fell.

'Before we finish, there is one other pet who deserves a particular mention for his bravery and quick-thinking today,' he said. 'And that is Archie, the salamander. Storm if you would like to bring Archie into the ring we have decided that we are

going to give him a special prize for
being our *favourite* pet!'

'Oh wow!' Storm gasped. 'Archie,
you've won a prize!'

'Go on!' Willow said, pushing him
into the ring.

The Tricorn presented Storm with
a special silver shield that Tor had
magicked. It had red ribbons tied on
both sides, and Storm held it in his
mouth very proudly.

'Well done, everyone!' the Tricorn said above the sound of cheering. 'Now, I am sure you would all like to go and see your parents and friends. Tea will be served in twenty minutes. Thank you!' He bowed his head and the pet show was over.

Storm and Troy came trotting out of the ring with Archie and Jet gambolling beside them.

'You both won trophies!' Willow cried. Whizzy chirruped loudly and flew around Storm and Troy's heads.

Storm looked delighted. 'Winning a trophy was great, but even if we hadn't won anything I'd have still thought that Archie was the best pet in the world! Thank you for finding me and making me come back and take him in the show.'

'That's OK, you'd have done the same for any of us,' Willow told him.

Troy nuzzled Jet. 'And though Archie's great, Jet's the best pet in the world!'

'No, Whizzy is,' said Willow.

'It's definitely Flutter,' said Sapphire.

'They're all the best!' declared Storm. 'And Unicorn School is the best school in the world.'

The others whinnied in agreement.

'The very best!' Willow said.